Weekly Reader Children's Book Club presents

BEN FINDS A FRIEND

by Anne-Marie Chapouton • pictures by Ulises Wensell

translated by Andrea Mernan

G. P. Putnam's Sons

New York

More than anything in the world, Ben wanted a pet that would be his friend. First, he asked his mother about a dog. A little brown dog with floppy ears and a wagging tail.

But his mother said, "I'm sorry, Ben, but dogs are too much trouble. They tear up the furniture. They bark at the neighbors. And you have to walk them every day."

So he asked his father about a cat. Just a small, purring
cat with soft, soft fur.

But his father said, "Oh, dear, Ben. Cats are terrible!
They scratch and bite and they steal food from the
refrigerator. I'm sorry but we just can't have a cat."

A few days later, Ben had an idea.
"How about a monkey?" he asked his mother.
"A small, funny monkey to play with me all
day long."

But his mother said, "A monkey! Don't be silly, Ben!
Monkeys are dirty and messy. And they have fleas. We
most certainly cannot have a monkey!"

Then Ben had another idea.

"Could we get a parrot?" he asked his father.

"Parrots don't have fleas, they don't steal food, and you don't have to take them out for walks. A nice blue and yellow parrot could talk to me all day long."

But his father said, "No parrots! They screech and squawk and say terrible things!"

The next morning, Ben had another idea.
"A hamster in a cage!" he called to his mother. "A
hamster is quiet and small. And I could take care of it
all by myself."

But his mother said, "Hamsters smell and they do
nothing but sleep all day. I don't like hamsters at all!"

Ben decided he would think of something else . . .
something very, very small.

But the next day, Ben couldn't get out
of bed. His head hurt. His throat hurt.
His stomach hurt.
"It's a bug," declared the doctor.
"Maybe it's come to keep me company."
Ben giggled.

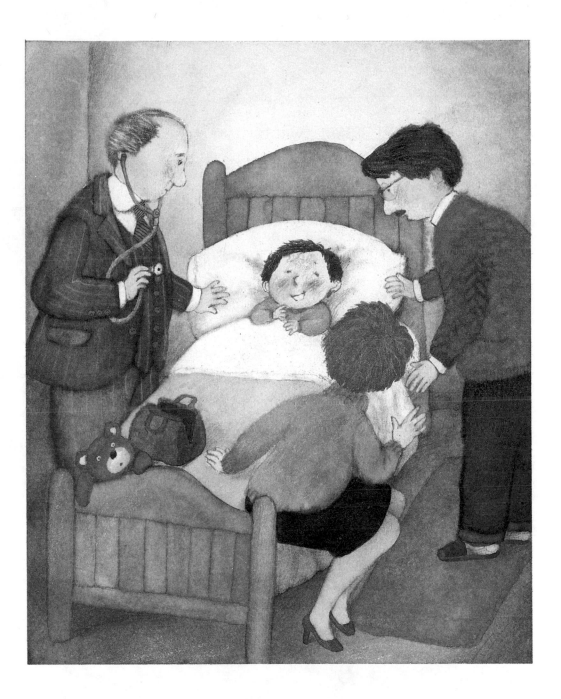

"When I grow up," Ben
decided, "things will be
different. I'll have all the
pets I want. I'll have a
friendly old turtle and big
fuzzy spiders that hang
from the ceiling."

"I'll keep a parrot in my closet, a hippo in the bathtub, and a giant snake will keep me company on the sofa."

The next morning Ben felt a little better. But he couldn't
think of any new ideas. "I'll never have a pet," he sighed.
And he felt all alone.

Until he heard a noise outside his window. "Coo, coo, coo."

On the windowsill was a big blue and gray pigeon. It
hopped along the sill, turned, and hopped back again. It
blinked and looked right at Ben. And then it flew away.

"I have an idea," said Ben.
And he asked his mother for some breadcrumbs.

"I think," Ben said, "I've finally found a friend."
And then he smiled and crawled back into bed.

Published by arrangement with G. P. Putnam's Sons.

Library of Congress Cataloging in Publication Data
Chapouton, Anne-Marie.   Ben finds a friend.
Originally written in French. Summary: Ben cannot think
of a pet his parents will let him keep in their apartment, until he finds an unexpected animal friend.
1. Children's stories, French. [1. Pets—Fiction.
2. Apartment houses—Fiction]   I. Wensell, Ulises, ill.
II. Title. PZ7.C3726Be   1986   [E]   85-3569
ISBN 0-399-21268-X